# The Spoon in the Stone

By Doug Peterson
Illustrated by Michael Moore

BIG IDEA
BOOKS

zonderkidz

BIG IDEA BOOKS®

www.bigidea.com

zonderkidz.
The children's group
of Zondervan

www.zonderkidz.com

*The Spoon in the Stone*
Copyright © 2005 by Big Idea, Inc.
Illustrations Copyright © 2005 by Big Idea, Inc.

Requests for information should be addressed to:
Zonderkidz, Grand Rapids, Michigan 49530

---

**Library of Congress Cataloging-in-Publication Data**

Peterson, Doug.
  The spoon in the stone / by Doug Peterson ; [illustrated by Big Idea, Inc.].
      p. cm. -- (VeggieTown values ; bk. 1)
  Summary: Junior Asparagus is reluctant to help a grouchy old neighbor, until a strange book transports him and Laura to Hamalot, where they become waiters and learn what it means to serve God by serving others.
    ISBN-10: 0-310-70626-2 (softcover)
    ISBN-13:978-0-310-70626-7
  [1. Waiters and waitresses--Fiction. 2. Knights and knighthood--Fiction. 3. Conduct of life--Fiction. 4. Vegetables--Fiction.] I. Big Idea, Inc. II. Title. III. Series.
    PZ7.P44334Spo 2005
    [Fic]--dc22
                                                                                            2004000462

---

Written by: Doug Peterson
Illustrated by: Michael Moore
Editor: Cindy Kenney
Art Direction & Design: Karen Poth

Printed in Hong Kong
05 06 07 08/PEH/7 6 5 4

"Anyone who wants to be important among you must be your servant."

(Mark 10:43)

# "Run, Junior, run!"

shouted Laura Carrot. "Leave the soccer ball behind!"

Junior Asparagus tore across Mr. Picklesheimer's backyard. Right behind him was a dog with ferocious fangs. The beast snarled and snapped.

Mr. Picklesheimer didn't like kids on his lawn so he bought a dog. Correction. He bought a creature that was part monster.

Junior ran for his life!

Just as the dog was about to attack, Junior leaped over the fence.  He was safe. But the soccer ball didn't make it. The dog tore it to pieces and gobbled it up.

Junior gulped. That soccer ball could have been him!

Junior's mom told him that everyone was going to help Mr. Picklesheimer!
"What?" exclaimed Junior.
"Mr. Picklesheimer is getting old, and he needs help doing his yard work.
So our family and the Carrots are going to help him. God wants us to serve
others, Junior."

"Today?" Junior gasped. "Laura and I have more important things to do!"

"There's nothing more important than serving others," Mr. Asparagus said. "We need you home by one o'clock."

Junior sighed. He didn't like this—**AT ALL**.

Junior and Laura complained loudly in the Treasure Trove Bookstore in the heart of VeggieTown.

"Why should we help a grouchy old pickle?" Laura muttered. "We have more important things to do."

Mr. O'Malley couldn't help but overhear. "Aye, you're having the same problem a lad and lassie had in a storybook I once read. Let's see if I can find it," said the Irish potato who owned the store.

"It's somewhere in the *Serving Others* section, right next to the Scratch-and-Sniff Classics," he mumbled. "Ahhh, here it is. It's called *The Spoon in the Stone*."

Junior opened to the first page and saw a huge castle with a draw-bridge. Standing in front of the castle were two Veggies in royal clothes.

Four words lifted up from the page into the air! They swirled around and around, growing larger and larger! Four simple words: **ONCE UPON A TIME.**

The four giant words swirled around Junior and Laura and...
**WHOOOOOOOOOOOOOOOOSHHHH!**
Junior and Laura found themselves falling
**down**
   **down**
     **down.**
   Everything was a blur as they zoomed straight through piles of
large words...and landed right in front of the castle door.

"Welcome to Hamalot!" shouted the tomato. "I'm Sir Irving, and this is my assistant, Sir Galaham. We run the Hamalot Hotel!"

"We like ham. **A LOT**," grinned the cucumber.

"We've been expecting you," said Sir Irving.

Junior and Laura blinked in surprise. "Huh?"

"Here's your apron," said Sir Galaham, "and your tray."

"Don't dilly-dally!" urged Sir Irving. "The hotel is packed with giants and ogres for this weekend's FE-FI-FO-FUN Trade Show. We have a shortage of servants!"

Irving and Galaham hurried them across a drawbridge. "There's much to do," Irving explained. "The Hamalot is the only place that leaves a ham on your pillow every evening instead of a mint."

Galaham grinned. "We like ham. **A LOT**."

"You can start on tables and deliver room service," explained Irving. He took Junior and Laura into the Hamalot Restaurant, which specialized in ham and beans, peanut butter and ham sandwiches, and banana-ham smoothies.

"You really do like ham. **A LOT**," observed Junior.

The restaurant was piled high with dirty dishes. Three lazy knights gobbled up food and played ping-pong with a hamball.

"That's Sir Nezzer, Sir Phillipe, and Sir Luntalot. They used to be hotel servants, but after they became knights, they decided they were too important to help around the hotel."

"These lazy knights used to be known as the Knights of the Round Table. But with no servants to clean up, the Round Table piled up with dirty dishes. So they switched tables and became the Knights of the Pool Table. Then they became the Knights of the Card Table. Now they're the Knights of the Ping-Pong Table," said Irving.

# At That Very Second...

A pea ran up to Sir Irving and handed him a slip of paper.

"Here's your first job!" Irving said. "We've got a rush order of ham and bean soup. Deliver it to Room 53!"

The Knights of the Ping-Pong Table suddenly stopped playing. The hamball bounced off of the table and clunked Sir Nezzer in the helmet. It knocked his visor shut, on his tongue.

"Outh."

"Room 53?" gasped Sir Phillipe. "That's the dreaded giant Grizzle's room."

"Grizzle is in the Deluxe Dungeon Suite," noted Sir Luntalot. "And he's very dangerous."

"Thath right," said Sir Nezzer, whose tongue was still caught.

Junior and Laura looked at each other. "Maybe we'd better not bother him."

"Nonsense," said Sir Irving as he handed the tray of food to Junior. "You'll be fine! Besides, if you don't serve him this food, Grizzle will tear apart our hotel."

# A Little While Later...

Laura knocked on the door to Room 53, and a giant pickle swung open the door. "WHAT TOOK YOU SO LONG?" he boomed.

If Junior had knees, they would've been shaking. A large dragon lurked behind the giant. Steam curled from its nose, which set off the smoke alarm.

The giant pickle roared and smashed the alarm into bits.

Junior cleared his throat and tried to be brave. "Your soup, sir."

The giant stared down at the bowl. "DA SPOON! WHERE'S DA SPOON?"

They forgot the spoon!

"I'll get it," Laura volunteered.

"*You* stay with *me*!" the giant roared. "If da little asparagus can't find da spoon before da Hamalot tower bell rings, den I'll have carrot stew instead."

Junior dashed back to the kitchen. All the spoons were caked solid with gunk!

"Please help me find a clean spoon!" Junior begged the Knights of the Ping-Pong Table.

"Sorry, we're knights, not servants," said Sir Luntalot.

"But God wants us to serve others!" Junior begged.

"Sorry," said Sir Nezzer. "We've got better things to do—like playing ping-pong."

Junior spotted a large spoon sticking out from a huge rock in the courtyard. He ran up to the spoon and grabbed the handle as the others gathered around him to see what would happen.

"That spoon is stuck in ancient oatmeal," explained Sir Galaham. "Many knights have tried to pull it out. But no one can do it."

Junior gave a mighty yank. The spoon wouldn't budge.

Then it happened. Junior gave a final tug, and the spoon slid from the stone, as smooth as butter. Trumpets sounded. Sunlight broke through the clouds. Everyone cheered!

Holding the spoon high like a sword, Junior dashed back into the hotel. But he was too late. The Hamalot tower bell was ringing.

After sprinting upstairs to Grizzle's room, Junior swung open the door. Was he too late to save his friend?

# He held his breath...

"Oh hi, Junior!" chirped Laura. "Mr. Grizzle and I are having tea."

"Huh?"

"After I gave Mr. Grizzle some tea, he calmed down," Laura continued. "He's really quite friendly."

Junior held out the golden spoon. "Your spoon, Mr. Grizzle."

Grizzle's eyes widened. "It's da *famous* spoon in da stone!"

"They say whoever pulls the spoon from the stone has a true servant's heart," Galaham explained.

"God wants us to be a servant to others," Junior smiled.

Later, in the courtyard, Sir Galaham asked Junior and Laura to kneel before him.

"I dub thee Sir Junior and Lady Laura," he said, gently tapping them on the head with the spoon.

"Hold it!" shouted Sir Phillipe. "By making them a knight and a lady, they'll be too important to be our servants!"

"Don't worry," Junior told them.

"There's nothing more important than serving others," Laura added. "Even when you're a knight."

Sir Galaham grinned. "I like that. **A LOT**."

# Just Then...

"Uh-oh," said Grizzle. "I think you're at **DA END** of da story."
"We'll miss you," Junior called.

# In a Blink...

They were back in the Treasure Trove Bookstore.

"Well, how did you like the book?" asked Mr. O'Malley, shuffling over to them with sandwiches and pink lemonade. "Learn anything about serving others?"

Junior and Laura stared at the old irish potato, still stunned by their adventure.

"Do **ALL** of your books do this?" Junior asked.

"Do what, laddie?" Mr. O'Malley asked as he set down the tray.

"You know. Pull you into the story?"

"Ahhh, all good stories pull you in," the potato said with a wink. "Here. Have a ham sandwich."

"Thanks," said Laura. "But we gotta get back home."

"Ahhh! That's right," agreed Mr. O'Malley. "You've got to help a neighbor, don't ya, lassie? But I thought you had more important things to do?"

Junior and Laura looked at each other.

"Nah," said Junior. "We can play later."

"Aye, that's the spirit!"

Mr. O'Malley watched as Junior and Laura dashed out the door. Then he sighed, took a big bite of ham sandwich, and smiled.

*I sure like ham*, he said to himself. ***A LOT.***

*In short, there's simply not
A more amazing spot
For happily serving other folks
Like a place called HAM-A-LOT!*